THE DAY
I HAD TO PLAY WITH
MY SISTER

THE DAY I HAD TO PLAY WITH MY SISTER

An Early I CAN READ Book

by CROSBY BONSALL

Harper & Row, Publishers
New York, Evanston, San Francisco, London

for Laura

THE DAY I HAD TO PLAY WITH MY SISTER

Copyright © 1972 by Crosby Bonsall

All rights reserved. No part of this book may be used or reproduced
in any manner whatsoever without written permission except in the
case of brief quotations embodied in critical articles and reviews.
Printed in the United States of America. For information address
Harper & Row, Publishers, Inc., 10 East 53rd Street, New York, N.Y.
10022. Published simultaneously in Canada by Fitzhenry & Whiteside
Limited, Toronto.
Library of Congress Catalog Card Number: 72-76507
Trade Standard Book Number: 06-020575-X
Harpercrest Standard Book Number: 06-020576-8

FIRST EDITION

Want to play a game?

You hide.

I will find you.

Okay?

One.

Two.

Three.

Here

I

come,

9

ready

10

or not.

THAT IS NOT THE WAY

TO PLAY THE GAME!

12

You HIDE, okay?

Hide in back of a tree.

14

Or hide here, see?

And I will find you. Okay?

15

One. Two. Three.

Here I come,

ready or not.

17

I know where you are.

I know. Here!

18

No, here!

No.

19

Well, I know

where you are.

20

You are

in the doghouse.

Now, you cut that out!

Hear?

This time I will hide.

You look for me, okay?

You say

one, two, three.

You say

here I come,

ready or not.

Okay?

Never mind.

I will hide.

You just look for me.

Now don't forget

to look

for me.

GET OFF MY LAP!

31

I don't want

to play with you

anymore.